Fairies

TO GEORGIA, A FRIEND OF THE FAIRIES

...when the first baby
laughed for the first time, the
laugh broke into a thousand pieces
and they all went skipping about, and
that was the beginning of fairies. And
now when every new baby is born, its first
laugh becomes a fairy. So there ought to
be one fairy for every boy or girl.

Peter Pan, J.M. Barrie

THIS IS A CARLTON BOOK

Design and text copyright © Carlton Books Limited 2009
Illustrations © Patricia Moffett 2009

This edition published in 2009 by Carlton Books Limited
An imprint of the Carlton Publishing Group
20 Mortimer Street
London W1T 3JW

10 9 8 7 6 5 4 3 2 1

First published in 2007 by Carlton Books Limited

A catalogue record is available for this book from the British Library.

ISBN: 978 1 84732 381 1

Printed and bound in China

Editor: Stella Caldwell
Creative director: Clare Baggaley
Project art direction: Zoë Dissell and Emma Wicks
Production: Lisa Moore

Fairies

Alison Maloney

Illustrated by Patricia Moffett

MADE WITH MAGIC
AND LOVE
BY CARLTON BOOKS

Fairyland

As children know, and adults rarely understand, *fairies are everywhere* – in your garden, in the woods beyond and even in your house! Although fairies can be found in every country in the mortal world, their true home is the far-off kingdom of Fairyland. This magical realm, which no human can ever reach, is the birthplace of all fairies.

The Magical Realm

Fairyland looks quite different from our world. The sky can change from blue to green in an instant, and the clouds look like candy floss. The streams and rivers run with shimmering gold, and the lakes contain pure dew water. Flowers of every description can be found throughout Fairyland – from roses and violets, to fantastical creations of silver and gold.

In the shops, the pixies sell fairy food, clothes and shoes alongside fairy dust, wands and ingredients for magic spells. A typical grocery store would be bursting with honey, dew-drop drinks and fruit, and would stock more herbs than you have ever heard of, with strange names like Mouse-ear Hawkweed, Hog's Fennel and Squirting Cucumber. Fairies use fairy gold for money, but beware the fairy that tries to sneak some out of Fairyland – it will instantly turn to dry leaves!

Fairyland is a lovely place to live and, for the most part, everybody gets along very well. Bad fairies are banished by Titania, queen of the fairies, and must be truly sorry before they can return. Those who are exceptionally good are granted a certificate of goodness, the highest honour the fairy queen can bestow.

LEAVING FAIRYLAND

Fairies are permitted to leave or are sent away by the queen, to do good work in the human world. Before travelling, they must sign a pledge to stay as far away from human adults as possible. Then they are questioned by the fairy council, and given written permission from the council and the queen. Fairies who leave Fairyland must return at least once a year to take part in the midsummer celebrations. Any fairy that leaves without seeking the queen's permission is banned from returning for a full seven years.

Departing fairies are given a splendid farewell party by their friends and families before heading off to the houses, gardens, woodlands and oceans of the human world.

The Fairy Queen's Castle

On top of a steep hill, *overlooking all of Fairyland, stands a magnificent fairy castle. Here lives Titania, queen of the fairies, and her husband Oberon, the fairy king. Beautiful and graceful, Titania is attended by flower fairy maids.*

Titania is kind and fair to her subjects. She often throws fantastic parties in the castle banquet hall, held on the full moon. Dressed in their most exquisite gowns and finery, the fairies feast on delicious fruits, berries, nectar and honey. When they can eat no more, they dance in the ballroom and by the light of the moon in the castle gardens, often until daybreak.

You spotted snakes with double tongue,

Thorny hedge-hogs, be not seen;

Newts, and blind-worms, do no wrong,

Come not near our fairy queen!

A Midsummer Night's Dream,
Shakespeare

THE FAIRY QUEEN'S RULES

1 A fairy must always be considerate to his or her fellow citizens.

2 Deliberate damage to property or nature's treasures will not be tolerated.

3 Animals are our friends and cruelty to them is an offence.

4 Jeering, mocking and bullying others because of their pointed ears, large nose or flat feet is strictly forbidden.

5 Litter should never be dropped in the streets and must be recycled in every instance.

6 Any item stolen by a resident will instantly turn to dust.

7 Tricks played on friends and neighbours must be merely mischievous, never malicious.

8 Fairies who leave the kingdom must return for the summer festivities, or will be unable to return for seven years.

9 Returning fairies must NEVER lead a human to Fairyland.

10 The queen must be obeyed at all times.

Magic and Mischief

Although they are playful creatures, *fairies are also hard workers. Most of them do their best to make the world beautiful, but a few naughty fairies put all their effort into playing tricks on humans.*

Magic Wands

Not all fairies carry wands but those that do are very careful never to lose them, as they can be dangerous in the wrong hands. The perfect wand is made from a hazel stick. It is whittled, which means the bark is cut away, and then a sparkling crystal is tied to the end. The wand is sprinkled with fairy dust to give it special powers. A fairy always writes her name, in invisible letters that only she can read, on the wood.

FAIRY GODMOTHERS

Most children have a fairy godmother to watch over them, although they rarely show themselves. Cinderella was lucky enough to meet hers otherwise she would never have made it to the ball. Sleeping Beauty was even luckier – she had six fairy godmothers to make sure the wicked fairy didn't get her way! If you should come across your fairy godmother, make the most of it. They are only given the power to help each person once, so make sure you ask for the right favour!

Fairy Ointment

This is a mysterious potion that fairies apply to the eyes of their newborn babies. It helps them to see magic which is never revealed to human eyes.

FOUR-LEAF CLOVERS

These tiny plants are extremely rare and very precious to fairies as they can be used to ward off bad spells. Humans consider them lucky too, so keep an eye out for one! The first leaf is said to bring hope, the second, faith and the third, love. The fourth leaf is for good luck.

Fairy Spades

These are smooth, slippery, black stones. When placed in the water they are said to cure sick animals and humans.

Fairy Dust

The most important of the work tools, a fairy will never travel without a special pouch of fairy dust. The ingredients are a secret that only the fairy king and queen, and the most important fairies are allowed to know, but it is thought that the dust falls from the moon and stars at night. It is usually gold or silver, although some of the flower fairies add ground petal to make it pink or purple. Fairy dust contains so much magic that the fairies' spells will work on anything it touches. This does mean that they have to be very careful where it lands!

Fairy Arrows

Arrows, or elf-bolts, are made from tiny pieces of flint and can be used by both good and bad fairies. They were once used by the woodland fairies to scare off hunters, but today they are used to deliver love potions or fairy medicine to needy humans. Some wicked fairies use them to make farm animals sick if a farmer has offended them.

CHANGELINGS

Changelings are fairy children that have been left in place of human babies so that the fairies may have a human servant. Changelings are usually bad-tempered, with a face which looks a bit like an old man or woman, and are exceptionally irritating. The only way of finding out whether your brother or sister is a changeling is to serve them dinner in an egg shell. If they are from the fairies they will cackle like an old man and speak as though they have lived for a hundred years. But don't worry, changelings are extremely rare!

House Fairies

Among all the fairies, *the house fairies are probably the most useful to humans. As in all fairy domains, there are those who are naughty and unhelpful, but, for the most part, the house fairies help with chores and look after the family. One thing these fairies have in common is the love of a clean house! They also need to be treated well – insult one and things could start to go wrong around the home…*

The Fairy Housekeeper

This friendly fairy helps to manage the housework and watches over the family. Mum and dad might notice the house looking extra clean, but would probably never suspect a fairy was at work! Each house will only have one fairy housekeeper, and they instruct brownies and silkies in their work. This fairy loves children and will often choose a warm, loving home to stay in, particularly if mum is tired and overworked. The fairy housekeeper will tuck children in and close windows if they are cold. She loves strawberries and cream, and will be delighted if you leave these out as a gift.

Silkies

The silkies are pretty fairies who dress in white or grey silk dresses. In the old days, when people had servants to do their chores, silkies would scold those who were not doing a good job. Nowadays, the silkies will do the chores themselves to help families who are too busy to clean properly. They can be very useful to forgetful people too, as they like to lead them to lost items such as keys or documents. However, unlike brownies, they have a mischievous side too and like to amuse themselves by jumping out of trees and scaring travellers!

Brownies

These cheerful little sprites are endlessly helpful and love to do the housework. They are not the prettiest of creatures, with flat faces and lots of hair, but they have the most enchanting smiles and friendly characters. They love to play with children and any child lucky enough to meet a brownie will be entertained with wonderful stories. The only thing that will drive your brownie away is a gift left out for them. This insults their good nature and they will never return, so beware!

Fairy Food

Nature provides all the food that fairies need – berries, fruit and honey. Fresh spring water helps to wash it down, although fairies that live on or near farmland love milk, straight from the cow. Fruit smoothies are a favourite treat, and for special occasions the fairies bake fairy cakes in a stone oven hidden in woodland caves.

A NAUGHTY HOUSE FAIRY

The boggart is not a welcome visitor in any home. Dirty and smelly gnome-like creatures, they wear wrinkled and dusty clothing. Extremely bad tempered, these fairies like playing nasty tricks, such as tipping over jugs and loudly slamming doors! Other favourite activities include tormenting dogs to make them bark and pulling the tails of cats. They are difficult to get rid of once they have moved in, but this can be done by making annoying noises such as banging pots and singing loudly.

Garden Fairies

Of all the world's fairies, *those found at the bottom of your garden tend to be the smallest. Their tiny size means that they can live close to humans – grown-ups are usually too busy to spot the tiny gardeners flitting about the flowerbeds. On the rare occasions they are spotted, it is usually by a child. After all, children take more notice of these things!*

Fairy Gardeners

Fairies that tend the garden flowers wake very early in the morning to make sure that the plants have had enough dew. They make sure that buds and blooms are coming through in the right colours, and can change them with fairy dust if they aren't quite right. They are incredibly beautiful and dress in delicate outfits made from fallen petals and leaves.

Pixies

Pixies are tiny winged creatures with pointed noses and ears, and they are very friendly and helpful. However, they enjoy playing pranks on humans, such as hiding trowels and making plants grow in funny directions! Pixies love to dance and gather together at pixie fairs. You can sometimes tell where they have met – they might leave behind a shimmering footprint, made from pixie dust.

Farm Fairies

On the more practical land of a farm, *the fairies are very different from the delicate creatures of the garden. The farm fairies are strong by nature and, therefore, able to help with the heavy work involved. However, the delicate farm elf deals with more gentle farm chores.*

Farmhands

Farmhand fairies ask only for a glass of milk in return for help with the farm work. The female, who has flowing blonde hair, travels from farm to farm to tend to cattle. As she travels by water, she arrives at the farm door soaking wet and asks to dry herself by the fire. If she is allowed in, she brings good luck to the family!

Portunes

These tiny fairies look like wrinkled old men! They are so small they can get through locked doors and appear in farmhouses at night to roast frogs on the fire. They have been known to annoy people by leading horses into marshes and bogs.

A Fairy Cobbler

The cheeky leprechaun is actually a fairy cobbler who makes shoes for a living, but he is happy to help out on a farm if need be. He may give the farmer a good luck charm, such as a four-leaf clover, and in return he will ask the farmer to make him tiny furniture, or provide leather for his shoes. Leprechauns love to have wild parties when the work is done. Legend has it that if a human is lucky enough to catch a leprechaun, he may be led to the end of the rainbow where a pot of gold awaits!

The Farm Elf

These are the smallest and the prettiest of the farm workers. They can be found helping milk turn to butter in the churn and giving the cheese its beautiful rind. They also like to look after the smaller farm animals, such as the chicks and lambs, but they keep well away from the farm cat!

Woodland Fairies

Forests and woods are perfect places *for shy little fairy folk to hide, and they are happiest living in unspoilt natural surroundings. Here, they are safe from the litter and noise of the human world, and from mortal eyes, especially those of the grown-ups.*

Woodland fairies enjoy each other's company and love to get together to share secrets and gossip! At night they gather to talk and dance, often at a spot with a circle of toadstools known as a fairy ring.

Gnomes

These wise guardians of mines and quarries are often found in forests. They love things that glitter, especially gem stones.

A Woodland Fairy's Day

Dawn: *Breakfast*

8am: *Meet others at the big oak tree*

9am: *Collect seeds from bluebells and forget-me-nots*

10am: *Scatter seeds throughout the wood*

1pm: *Lunch*

2pm: *Collect petals*

4pm: *Make petal perfume*

6pm: *Find new ferns for beds*

7pm: *Home for dinner*

10pm: *Put on dancing shoes for the fairy meeting!*

Wood Nymphs

These fairies live in trees and will only stay alive as long as their tree does. They are very beautiful and kind but will get angry if their homes are damaged. They love to see children climbing and having fun with trees, but do make sure you never break off a branch!

THE BLUEBELL FESTIVAL

The most important day of the woodland
fairy calendar is the Bluebell Festival, which
is held in spring when the bluebells bloom.
The beautiful carpet of flowers provides a
lovely setting for this magical fairy festival,
and the little folk gather from miles
around to celebrate. Hundreds of fairies,
in shimmering dresses and their best
waistcoats, dance through the night
to mark the end of the
long, hard winter.

BUTTERFLY FAIRIES

Beautiful and extremely rare, these
fairies have the coloured wings of
butterflies. They live deep
in the forest, and feed on
flower nectar and honey.
They are so shy, they
are hardly ever
spotted.

Woodland Sprites

Sprites love water and are usually
found near a stream or lake. They
can be mischievous, but they are not
spiteful. In the autumn, it is their
job to paint the leaves different
shades of yellow and red.

Work and Play

During the day, woodland fairies work hard and spend their time looking
after flowers, trees and plants, as well as animals. Squirrels and mice are
their friends, and these creatures are happy to let tired fairies ride on their backs.

Woodland fairies love midnight picnics. They are fond of
nuts, acorns and berries, such as blackberries, but their
favourite food is honey! Pixies collect this wonderful
substance from their friends, the bees, and
bring it to the woodland fairies.

Water Fairies

Water has magical qualities *and attracts many types of fairy. Whether they live in vast seas, tranquil lakes or tiny streams, the water fairies look after the plants, fish and many other creatures that share their underwater homes.*

Glastigs

Female water sprites, known as Glastigs, have the faces and bodies of beautiful women and the hooves of goats. These fairies love music and help women and children who are in trouble, but they can be dangerous to human men, luring them into traps with sweet music and dancing.

Water Nymphs

Beautiful water nymphs watch over fountains, springs, wells and streams. Each nymph stays with her own spring or stream, nourishing the surrounding land and crops, and helping plants to grow. These fairies can give water special healing powers. Those who drink from a fountain or well which is home to a water nymph will soon find that good luck comes their way!

Asrai

Small and beautiful, Asrai fairies are hard to spot as they are afraid of sunlight and are so delicate you can see right through them! They live in the deep blue seas and only come to the surface on moonless nights, once every hundred years.

THE FISHERMAN AND THE ASRAI

Long ago, when a full moon shone bright, a fisherman pulled in his nets to find a beautiful creature caught in the mesh. The Asrai begged him to release her, but her voice sounded like the waves, and he didn't hear. She pleaded with her eyes, but the fisherman was greedy, and thought he could make money from this wondrous creature.

When he reached the shore, the fisherman gathered the townsfolk together to take a look at his beautiful captive. However, when he moved the net, all he found was a puddle of water. He thought that perhaps he had dreamed everything. But, as the years went by, and whatever the weather, a spot on his arm where the Asrai had touched him remained icy cold.

Water Sprites

These tiny fairies look like human females, but have hair as blue as the sea in which they live. They are able to breathe in both air and water, and are friendly unless threatened. They are happy to help humans in danger, and have been known to rescue fishermen who have fallen overboard.

THE LADY OF THE LAKE

You may have heard of King Arthur and his famous sword, Excalibur. It was given to him by the fairy queen Viviane, also known as the Lady of the Lake. A water fairy with vast powers, the Lady of the Lake gave the king the enchanted sword to protect him in battle. When he was finally wounded, Excalibur was thrown back into the misty waters and the Lady was seen rising above the water to reclaim it.

Fairy Homes

Fairies choose their homes very carefully. *For those who live in Fairyland, there is no problem finding the perfect home. However, for garden, woodland and water fairies, it can be difficult finding the ideal abode.*

House Hunting

Fairy homes need to be in a pretty setting hidden from inquisitive human eyes. They are always built in sheltered areas, as fairies prefer not to get wet (unless they are water fairies, of course!). The places they choose must be clean, as fairies hate litter. Many a fairy has been forced to leave their home because of careless litterbugs.

Garden fairies often build a tiny home from twigs and leaves. Woodland fairies prefer the hollow of a tree, or the inside of a very large toadstool. You might find a fairy ring, which is a circle of toadstools, used by the tiniest woodland fairies.

Leprechauns often live hidden away in the cellars of houses or in the corner of a barn. Dream and tooth fairies always live in Fairyland, in sugar-pink houses around the chief tooth fairy's palace. Beautiful water fairies live in shimmering coral caves decorated with mother of pearl and seashells.

Famous Fairies

When the name of a fairy is known throughout the world, *the fairy queen grants him or her a place in the Fairyland Hall of Fame. This long gallery contains portraits of the most famous fairies in history. The good ones get pride of place in the gallery, while the bad fairies' portraits hang in a dark corner.*

Thumbelina and Tom Thumb

Thumbelina was a beautiful, tiny fairy child who emerged from a flower and was brought up by a human woman. Kidnapped by a frog who wanted a bride for her son, Thumbelina escaped with the help of a butterfly but was then stolen away by a mayfly! After many adventures Thumbelina was finally delivered to a handsome fairy prince on the back of a bird.

Like Thumbelina, Tom Thumb was a fairy child, no bigger than a thumb, who was raised by human parents. He was very accident-prone and often fell into animal troughs and pots, but he used his fairy magic to escape each danger.

The Blue Fairy

If it wasn't for the beautiful Blue Fairy, Pinocchio, a mischievous little puppet, would never have become a real boy!

Brave Pinocchio! In return for your good heart I forgive you all your past misdeeds.

The Blue Fairy, Pinocchio, Carlo Collodi

The Christmas Fairy

The Christmas Fairy is part of Santa's team of helpers and she helps him create the lists of presents for each child. When the Christmas decorations go up, the Christmas Fairy leaves the North Pole and looks after Christmas trees all over the world. If she doesn't watch over them, they might lose their pine needles before Christmas day, which would never do!

The Sleeping Beauty Fairies

Sleeping Beauty had six fairy godmothers who tried to protect her from their sister, the wicked fairy. The wicked fairy cast a spell that Sleeping Beauty would prick her finger on her sixteenth birthday, and die. However, one of the good fairies used her magic to soften the curse so that the princess wouldn't die but instead fall into a deep sleep that would last for a hundred years. Sure enough, these things came to pass. It was a hundred years before a handsome prince was able to rouse the princess with a kiss!

The Snow Queen

This fairy queen was bewitchingly beautiful, but she had a cold and wicked heart! Anybody who was kissed by her three times would instantly be turned to ice.

Tinker Bell and Neverland

The most famous fairy of all, Tinker Bell, was Peter Pan's own fairy. She was given her name because she fixed pots and kettles, like a tinker, and her voice sounded like a bell. Tinker Bell was no bigger than a hand but she was very beautiful. She flitted around very fast and appeared as a tiny light in the dark. She could be very bad-tempered, but was devoted to Peter and protected him from the evil Captain Hook.

Tinker Bell lived in a place called Neverland and shared her home with the Lost Boys, a group of children who never grew up. Pirates, mermaids and Red Indians also lived in Neverland, which can only be reached by flying past a certain star...

The fur coat and the cap were made of snow, and it was a woman, tall and slender and blinding white – she was the Snow Queen herself.
The Snow Queen, Hans Christian Andersen

Second to the right and straight on till morning...

The Tooth Fairy

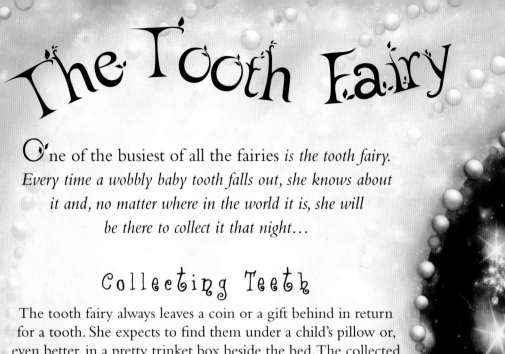

One of the busiest of all the fairies *is the tooth fairy. Every time a wobbly baby tooth falls out, she knows about it and, no matter where in the world it is, she will be there to collect it that night…*

Collecting Teeth

The tooth fairy always leaves a coin or a gift behind in return for a tooth. She expects to find them under a child's pillow or, even better, in a pretty trinket box beside the bed. The collected teeth are kept in a huge store room at the palace. A special assistant works permanently in the tooth library where the names of all the children in the world are stored. Fairies travel from near and far to buy the teeth and the pretty jewellery that the tooth fairy's elf friends make from them.

The tooth fairy is one of the smallest and prettiest of her kind, and takes great trouble with her appearance. She wears shimmering white gowns and beautiful jewellery, made from the purest of baby teeth. Her pearl slippers are made from spun white silk, her wings shimmer with a golden glow and her hair shines as if it is laced with glitter. She always carries a gold silk purse with her, full of her own special fairy dust. Should a child begin to stir while she is collecting her treasures, she can send them back to sleep with one pinch of this magical substance.

Travelling the World

How does the tooth fairy know where she is nee every night? During the day, while the tooth fai sleeps, sprite spies travel the world looking for children with wobbly teeth. If it looks like a tooth's about to pop out, the sprites write the child's name in a special log book.

When the tooth fairy awakens, she checks the names in the log book and works out her collection round for the night ahead.

The Dream Fairies

Along with the sprite spies and helpful elves, the tooth fairy works closely with the dream fairies. In fact, when an aging tooth fairy decides to retire (flying around the world every night is very tiring after all!), a new one is chosen from the dream fairies. Dream fairies also work only at night and sleep during the day. Their job is to banish nightmares and make sure children are tucked up in bed, warm and cosy, and having sweet dreams. Should they come across a child who is having a bad dream, they can take the dream away and blow it up to the skies, where it evaporates to form a small black cloud. When the small clouds mix together to form a big heavy cloud, the nightmares are turned into rain, washing all bad thoughts away.

SWEET DREAMS

★ Always go to bed when your parents tell you to – you don't want to keep the dream fairies waiting!
★ Think lovely thoughts as you put your head on the pillow. Holidays, beaches and best friends are the most perfect dreamy thoughts.
★ Just in case they are listening, it's a good idea to say "Goodnight dream fairies". They do love to be welcomed into a room!

Fairy Fashions

Fairies are very fashion conscious *and love to look their best, especially at their nightly meetings. Using spider silk, colourful petals and pretty leaves, fairies are very creative at making clothes and jewellery from nature's treasures.*

Nature's Treasures

Spider silk is the most beautiful and delicate material, and is in plentiful supply in woods, gardens and houses. It is also very strong and elastic. Spiders are happy to spin for their fairy friends as are moth caterpillars. Ants, bees and wasps are also able to make silk, which they use for nest-building. A fairy who helps busy insects, collecting nectar or building homes, will be rewarded with the rarest of silk. This is very special and is normally saved for making ball gowns.

Petals and leaves are often used for fairy outfits, particularly those of the flower and woodland fairies. Fairies always have a sparkling new outfit for for the midsummer celebrations, which last throughout the longest day of the year.

ACCESSORIES

Fairies love pretty things and always complete their outfits with matching accessories. Brightly coloured jewellery is made from dried seeds and berries, or from gems and crystals which are mined by the elves and strung together with the finest spider silk. Water fairies make their trinkets from coral and pearls, and they love mother-of-pearl shells with their swirling colours of silver and pink.

For footwear, the fairies rely mainly on leprechauns, the fairy cobblers. Leprechauns can sew the daintiest shoes as well as making the sturdy boots that elves wear. Silk is used for bags and crushed petals provide coloured dye for the fabric. Bags and hats can also be made from petals or whole flowers, as well as walnut and hazelnut shells, fastened with a clasp of vine. Colourful feathers, glued on with beeswax, make charming additions to the hats.

FAIRY WINGS

In Fairyland, wings are seen as the ultimate fashion statement but not all fairies are born with them. Flightless fairies often possess several pairs of wings which they wear for special occasions. These are spun from the finest gossamer and are attached to threads which can be tied over the shoulders. They can also be made from feathers, shed by young birds as they learn to fly.

Seasonal Dressing

In order to stay hidden, fairies try to blend into the background. Many types, particularly woodland fairies, change their clothing to reflect the changing seasons.

Spring

As nature awakens in a riot of blue and green, the fairies celebrate by sewing beautiful ball gowns in preparation for the Bluebell Festival. Daffodil yellow, tulip pink and, of course, bluebell blue are the colours of the season!

Autumn

As leaves and petals fall from the trees in shades of red, green and orange, the elf tailors are busy making them into autumn outfits. Acorn shells lined with soft feathers make comfortable hats and the fallen conker shells are used to make umbrellas.

Summer

As this is the most colourful season of the year, fairies take the opportunity to dress in vibrant pinks and purples, to echo the many blooming flowers. Their outfits are skimpy at this time of year, as they do not like to be too hot, and they often wear petal sunhats.

Winter

White spider silk and rabbits' hair are woven together to make warm coats for the fairies and blankets for the babies. Farm fairies and those that live near sheep collect tufts of wool from the fences and bushes, which is woven into felt to line their boots. Ivy-leaf shawls are popular for eveningwear at this time of year.

Fairy Foes

Most fairies put their magic to good use, *but they have to be very careful as they have some enemies. Grown-up humans can cause problems for the fairies, mainly by destroying the places where they live. However, those creatures that possess similar magical powers to the good fairies, but use them for wicked purposes, pose the greatest danger. The worst among these are the witches, goblins and trolls who do their best to spoil the fairies' good work.*

Witches

These cave-dwelling hags often live in woodland where fairies live – and oh, how they hate them! They use their magic to trap fairies, imprisoning them in bottles so they can steal their fairy dust. A pinch of fairy dust added to a witch's cauldron makes her spell twice as powerful. Really wicked witches have been known to put a whole fairy in the pot if she refuses to surrender her dust!

However, some witches have come to see the error of their ways after meeting a particularly good fairy. These "white witches" can use their spells to help others.

THE FROST GIANTS

The frost giants live in Niflheim, a land of eternal cold, and are the enemies of the elves and fairies.

The first frost giant was called Ymer and was formed when the cold air of Niflheim met the warm air of the neighbouring land of fire and embers. As Ymer slept his body grew in size and a whole race of giants was born.

The giants are huge beings who can freeze everything for miles around and use their powers to destroy the marine life, plants and flowers that the fairies work so hard to protect. They often take the form of a freezing fog to move across the land, destroying wildlife in their path. The layer of frost left on objects after a freezing fog could mean that a giant has passed that way. They rarely harm humans, though – for one thing they would melt if they entered a human house!

Goblins

Sometimes called hobgoblins, these short stocky men are at war with the fairies. They are so ugly that they envy the prettier fairy races and often attempt to exchange their own hideous babies with those of the beautiful fairies. Goblins particularly hate elves, and will fight with them whenever they meet. A goblin's smile can turn milk sour and their magic can create fire! This makes them extremely dangerous to the fairies whose wings are easily burnt.

Trolls

Fairies are very frightened of the ugly ogre-like creatures that guard the bridges of the hills and mountains. Trolls are usually green in colour and, although they eat goats, they are unlikely to harm people, preferring to scare them instead. They do dislike fairies, though, and will squash them with their huge hands if they get the chance. Luckily most fairies are too quick for these stupid, lumbering creatures so, while they may get a scare, they usually escape unharmed.

Finding Fairies

You may have fairies *at the bottom of your garden or even in your house, but they are very shy and use magic to hide themselves. If you are very lucky, though, you might find clues that a fairy has left behind. Children are much better at spotting these signs than grown-ups. Keep your eyes and ears open, and who knows what you might find. Good luck!*

In the House

House fairies are extremely tidy creatures so they are careful to clear up any signs of their presence. Sometimes a little drop of milk or breadcrumbs in the kitchen means the fairies have been having a meal. When your cat seems very interested in something under the cupboard, or the dog seems restless, it may be because they have seen a fairy. If an animal starts chasing its tail, it may be because it has an invisible rider!

In the Garden

Look under the bushes in the garden and see if you can find a pile of leaves or petals. A fairy may have slept there. A row or a circle of stones can mean a midnight meeting has taken place, as they are often used as seats.

FAIRY RINGS

At night, fairies have been spotted dancing in woodland where they leave small circles known as fairy rings. Never go in search of these night-time dances on your own – their magic can be very powerful. The enchanting music tempts people to come close, but you must always watch from afar. People who have been lured too close to fairy rings have told strange stories of how the dance seemed to last only for a few moments, when in fact they disappeared from their human lives for a whole seven years!

In the Woods

The most obvious sign that fairies are living in the woods is a ring of toadstools. Dances and meetings take place at fairy rings and toadstools make perfect fairy seats! If you find a hollow tree, take a peek inside. Any piles of leaves, acorns or twigs may well have been left there by fairies.

ATTRACTING FAIRIES

The best time to attract good fairies is when the moon is full. This is a very magical time.

Some flowers have special properties. Sunflowers, nasturtiums and tulips are all garden fairy favourites, and are likely to draw them near. Fruits, such as strawberries provide them with food, while sweet-smelling flowers, such as lavender and honeysuckle, will attract them from further away. Building a fairy house and leaving tiny cups of water inside is a lovely way of making the fairies feel welcome.

The best possible way of attracting house fairies is to keep everything clean! Untidy bedrooms will have these fairies scooting off into the night, and dust and dirt will only attract bad fairies. Leave tiny portions of honey, milk and cake on your window sill.

A rustle in the wind reminds us a fairy is near...

Certificate of Fairydom

This is to certify that

....

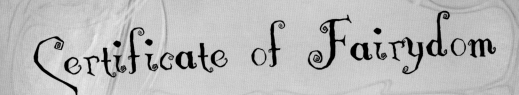

Place your
photograph
here

is now a keeper of fairy secrets.

From this day forth, by royal command, she shall be recognized
as a trusted friend of fairy folk and will swear never to
reveal her knowledge to the grown-up ones.

Queen Titania

CONGRATULATIONS!

You have learned all the secrets of the fairy kingdom and are now officially a friend of all fairies.

As a reward, I am awarding you a certificate to prove that you have earned the trust of fairy folk. Remember, the fairy secrets are now in your care. Keep them well.

With love and magic,

Queen Titania

Faeries, come take me out of this dull world,
For I would ride with you upon the wind,
Run on the top of the dishevelled tide,
And dance upon the mountains like a flame

"The Land of Heart's Desire", W.B. Yeats

The End